❧ **Thank you** ❧

to my parents for always believing in me;

to friends, family, and strangers that supported this project;

to my musical mentor Paul Fowler for giving me the tools and confidence;

to Katherine Breen for going above and beyond illustrating my vision.

And Thank You to all the musicians

that poured their heart and soul

to bring Water Wings to life.

To Jonah Bear, Follow your heart!
♡ Gah-bé

♡ Katherine Breen

❧ FIRST EDITION ❧

This book is written in Song Form
and uses different grammar.

Go to **waterwingsproductions.com** to download the musical audiobook accompaniment. Flip the pages and follow along to get the full immersive musical experience.

For more information contact waterwingsproduction@gmail.com

ISBN-13: 978-1-7332373-0-7
printed in China

Water Wings

the musical storybook experience

Written by **Gabriel Vanaver**   Illustrated by **Katherine Breen**

Once upon a coral reef, there lived a Little Fish

Comfortable in her little corner of the sea,

No cares, no worries, swimming free

Living her fishy life naturally

No other place she would rather be.

And so she swam her daily swim
Amidst the seaweed with her little fishy friends.
Tides rose and fell, rocking the kelp,
Crustaceans clicked away tapping their shells,
Sweet songs were heard from the dolphins and whales.

One day in school, Little Fish became a little curious.

Professor Water Snake was teaching about the ebb and flow.

"Our life force is getting toxic, and times are changing

And the water spirits are getting furious.

What can we do? How can we continue to grow?"

Little Fish thought about it all afternoon
Awakening to these changes all around.
The coral less colorful, the water less clear,
To see the sea like this brought her to tears.
All her surroundings were now shaken and unsound.

But as she lay down to rest in her little fishy nest, she thought,

"Well, I have been okay so far. How different can things get?"

With peace of mind, sound asleep

She dreamt of her perfect world beneath.

Little did she know, her life was about to change.

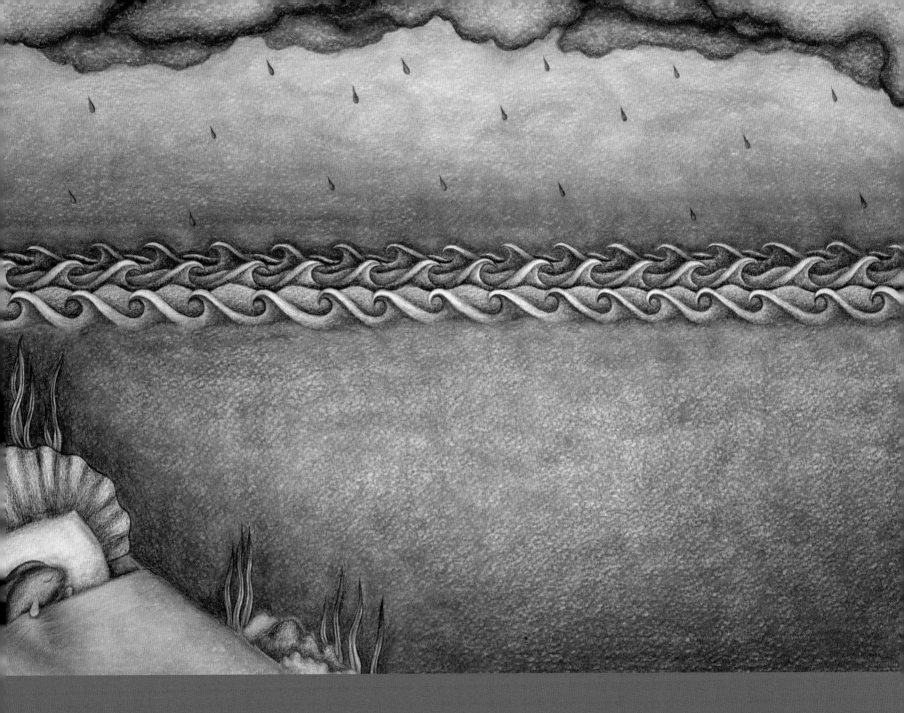

Pitter patter on the water, raindrops began to drum!

Pitter patter on the water, raindrops began to drum!

Waves began to rage, the water was wild

An endless storm for miles and miles.

From out of the blue, this terrible storm had come!

All the reef residents, a-frantic, swim around
Trying to hold their homes in the ground
But Little Fish, dreaming her wonderful dream,
Slept all through the night—la la dee
Tuning out the noises of the sea.

As the waves welled and crashed on the surface
Currents rushed all through the reef
Scooping up Little Fish, bed and all!
The water carried her far, far away
Taking her out to the deep blue sea
Taking her out, out to the deep blue sea.

Confused and alone, Little Fishy swam on
Broken home, lost at sea
So she stopped all the creatures she passed
Asking and pleading her story.
"Excuse me, Sea Turtle. Could you point me toward the shallows?"
"Shallow, deep. What difference does it make?"
"Excuse me, Sir Tuna. Which way to the shore?"
"Which shore? What shore? This shore, that shore? Hmm. I'm not quite sure."

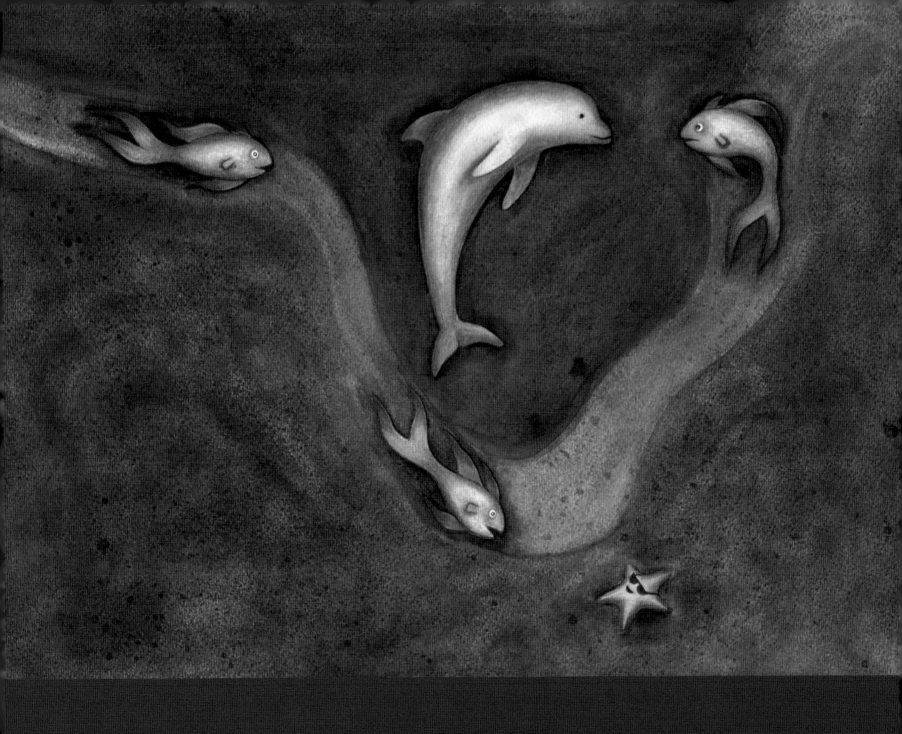

"Excuse me, Ms. Starfish. I am lost. Could you tell me where I am?"

"I'm sorry, Little Fish, but I can barely see. All I know is where I am."

"Excuse me, Dolphin. What am I to do? I'm cold. I'm lost. What do I do now?"

"Do what you want. Go where you will. The whole world is your playground!"

Unbeknownst to the Little Fish,

A shark silently sliced through the water

With eyes wide and hungry, licking his lips

He meant to make Little Fish his dinner.

"No one understands! My life was so perfect.

I was living how I was meant to live."

Upon hearing this Little Fish's story,

Mr. Shark began to cry...

"I once had a life like yours.

A perfect life, with family and friends.

Now I roam these dark waters

From meal to meal, to no end.

Just go! Just get! Be on your way!

You're too little to eat anyway.

Follow your dreams.

You'll find your way through.

Just go where the water takes you."

So deeper and deeper into the blue

Little Fish went where the currents carried her to.

The deeper she went, the rougher the waves

And her little fins were just no match.

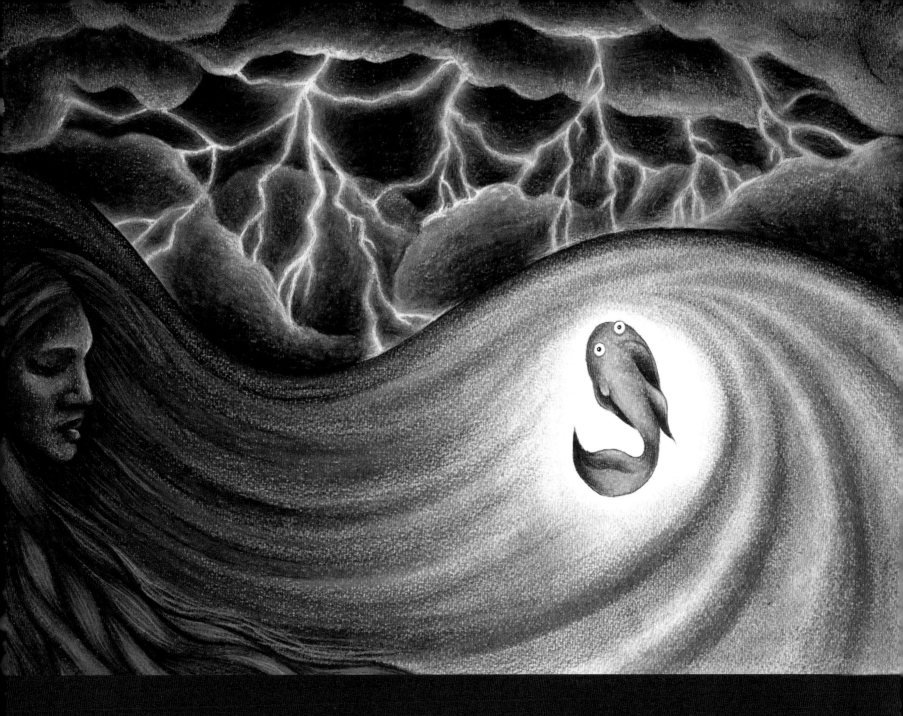

All hope lost, Little Fishy gave up

Weeping to the sea.

Lightning cracked and the ocean awoke

To listen to the Little Fish's plea.

Amidst the chaos, Little Fish found herself
suspended in a calm bubble of water
and out of the blue, a voice spoke.
"I have been watching you, and I hear your cry.
I know it seems as though there is nothing left to do.
You are not alone. There are countless others just like you!
Fear not, Little Fish, I will show you."

Little Fish realized this was a water spirit that held her!

With that, the water spirit spread its water wings

The waters raged all around them

as they climbed the hurricane.

They spun up through a cyclone.

Up and up they went, whirling and spinning...

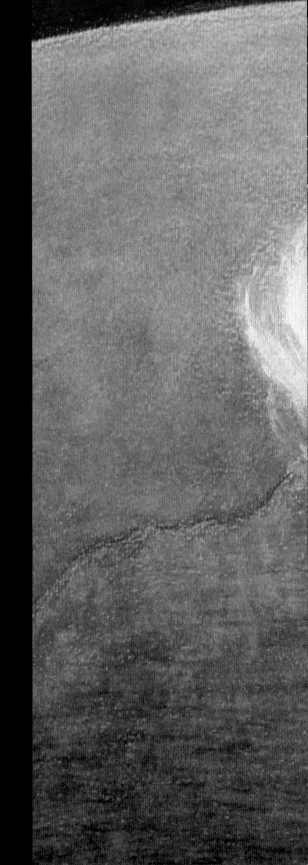

…until they rose up above the storm

Little Fish could see so very far,

she could almost see the curve of the earth.

"Look all around—

This whole world is where you live,

Filled with lifeforms, all shapes and sizes.

So many paths,

So many roads,

Where to go?

But there is one thing that we all must follow."

They rode the storm over land, where they witnessed the hurricane's destruction

All manner of creatures ran and hid, no choice but to survive.

"How awful," Little Fish thought, "Is this what I must see?"

Still in wonder, they continued on their journey.

"In every creature, I am within
Surging and coursing through their veins,
Coming and going, flowing and growing,
I am the cycle of change."
They rumbled with the dark clouds past the shores,
reaching as far inland as they could...

...And they dove with the rain.

"Ever falling, ever flowing, ever growing

No way to control, no way of knowing

Where to be, and when to be going

We must watch and listen close to our surroundings."

They splashed into a puddle

and seeped deep beneath the earth

where they fed the seeds, trees, shrubs,

and entire forest.

"Follow you heart at your pace

And all will fall into place.

Let the flow be your guide,

I am always at your side.

In all aspects of life,

There are ups and there are downs.

We ebb, we flow, high and low.

There is no limit, no one way to live it.

We are alive, so we adapt and change.

We are alive, so we adapt and change."

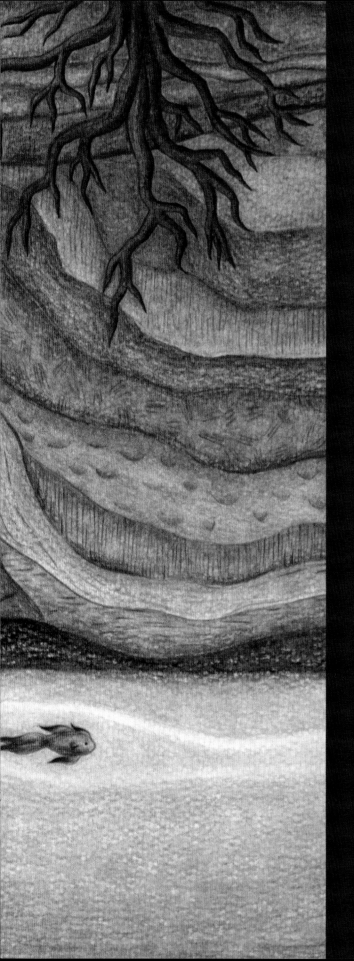

"We all have this power to transform.

Just look at me!

I once was dirty, angry, toxic rain,

But as I filter through this earthen soil

I am fresh once again."

They drip into a cave

and emerge out of a mountain spring.

"Life was never meant to be easy.

Through these hardships

We find our passion for life.

With every experience,

Do not fear and run away.

There is always something new,

Each and every day."

As they begin to travel down the river they watch as everything springs to life.

They watch as all manner of beings drink of this water.

People begin rebuilding their homes and beavers gather logs

and driftwood for their dams.

"You see Little Fish, we are adapting

Rising above what has happened, and rebuilding,

Look at the birds gather fallen branches to build their nests,

As a tree breaks and falls, it could mean a home for others to rest."

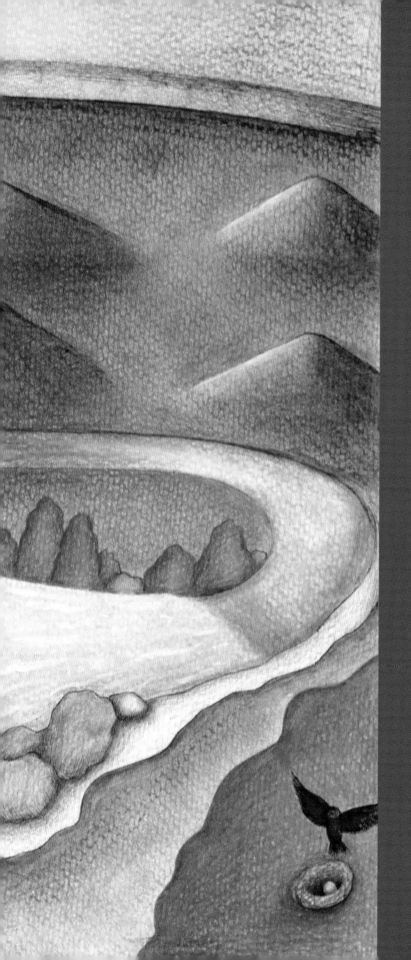

And they fall with the waterfall

and watch the beauty of the world

shine around them.

"Do you see now

How the cycle of nature is sewn?

By every way we imagine,

Life does flourish.

Everyone thrives from water,

Every shape and form,

Rivers to hurricanes.

Water awakens to this nature of change.

We are all made of water,

So we must adapt

And flow with the current."

They come to a bend in the river,
where they find an Old Man sitting under a tree,
playing his guitar and singing the blues.

"I've lived longer than most, as you may be able to tell.
I've seen so many heavens, and far too many hells.
Through all of these seasons, I've tried to find the reasons,
What keeps me going, who knows?
What keeps me going, who knows?

One thing I can say is life is a funny thing.
You never can tell what the next moment will bring.
So loosen up that grip, though it may feel strange
And let life grab you for a change.
Let go and let life grab you for a change.

Do not twist these words my friend.
Don't let anything tell you that you have reached the end.
You got to get up, make your own ripples in the waves
And dance with life, that's the essence of change
Dance with life, that's the essence of change
Dance with life, that's the essence of change
Dance with life, that's the essence of change..."

Little Fishy began to smile

for the first time since her journey began.

She realized what she must do.

She danced downstream

following the water spirit back to the sea.

She was brought back to her little reef

and the spirit let her go.

Little Fishy thanked the water spirit

for showing her the world

and giving her inspiration to rebuild.

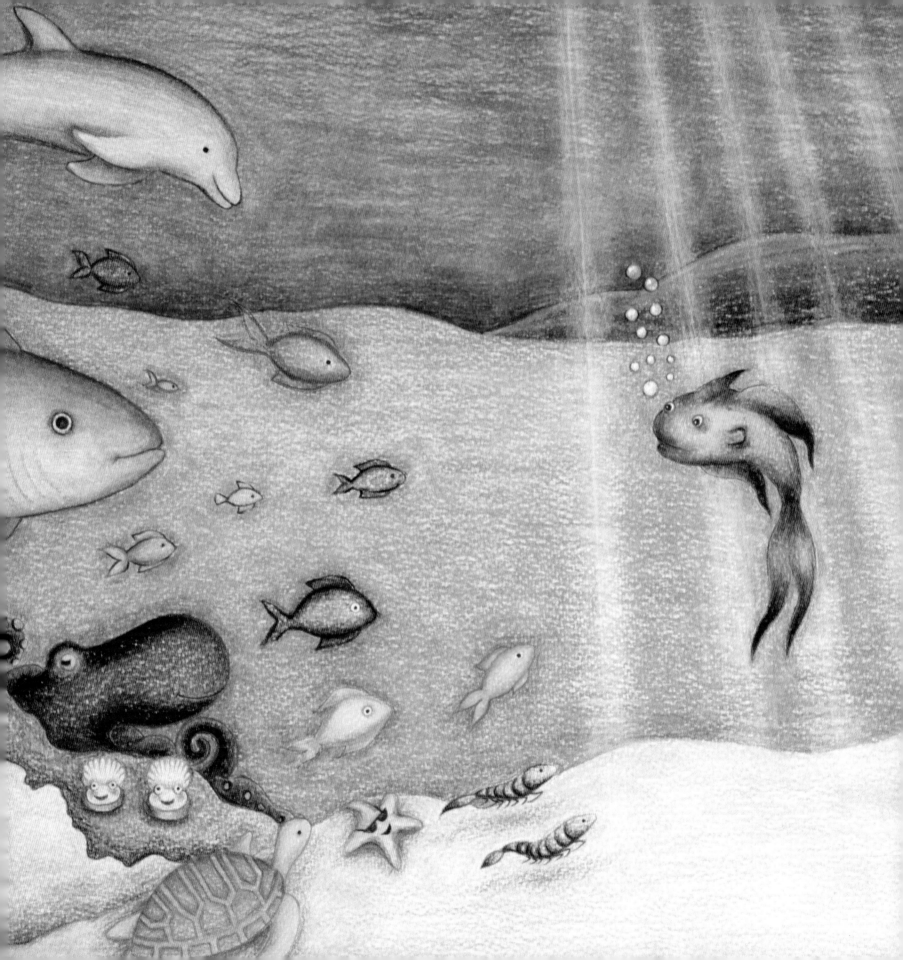

She then gathered her reef together
and taught them all that she had learned.

"Life gives and life takes away.
That's just the way it is.
No point on dwelling on what could have been.
When one thing ends, another begins.

Follow your heart and all will fall into place.
Follow your heart and all will fall into place..
Follow your heart and all will fall into place.
Follow your heart and all will fall into place..

Things fall apart, we must come together
To rebuild our life and help one another.
Each time we fall, we rise a bit stronger
And rebuild our life even better.

Just follow your heart, and all will fall into place.
Follow your heart and all will fall into place..
Follow your heart, and all will fall into place.
Follow your heart and all will fall into place..
Follow your heart, and all will fall into place.
Follow your heart and all will fall into place.."

And so all the reef residents scuttled along

rebuilding their homes as they whistled this song

and Little Fish nestled into a new, better home

carved by the current that once carried her away.

And as she lay down to rest,

she let her dreams take flight

and flow like the water.

Credits

Written by **Gabriel "Gah-bé" Vanaver**

Illustrated by **Katherine Breen**

Music Produced by **Gabriel Vanaver, Evan Reeves and Dango Rose**

Engineered by

Evan Reeves
Max Nordby
Jackson Prince
Patrick Tracy
George Lacson
Gabriel "Gah-bé" Vanaver

Recorded at Elephant Collective Studios
in association with UI Sound Studios in Boulder, CO

Featuring the Voices of

Narrator - **Gabriel "Gah-bé" Vanaver**
Little Fish - **Bridget Law**
Water Spirit - **Xerephine**
Old Man - **Guy Davis**
Shark - **Dango Rose**
Professor Water Snake - **William Sacks**
Sea Turtle - **Carlo Suits**
Tuna - **Kati Bicknell**
Starfish - **Katherine Breen**
Dolphin - **Paul Fowler**

PART ONE

"Once Upon a Coral Reef"

Narrator - **Gabriel "Gah-bé" Vanaver**
Little Fish - **Bridget Law**
Professor Water Snake - **William Sacks**

Guitar - **Evan Reeves**
Mandolin & Upright Bass - **Dango Rose**
Fiddle - **Bridget Law**
Percussion - **Darren Garvey**

PART TWO

"Lost at Sea"

Narrator - **Gabriel "Gah-bé" Vanaver**
Little Fish - **Bridget Law**
Professor Water Snake - **William Sacks**
Sea Turtle - **Carlo Suits**
Tuna - **Kati Bicknell**
Starfish - **Katherine Breen**
Dolphin - **Paul Fowler**
Shark - **Dango Rose**

Musical Performance by The Super Saturated Sugar Strings
feat. Phil Norman (Cello), Dango Rose (Upright Bass) & Darren Garvey (Percussion)

===

PART THREE

"Expanding Horizons"

Narrator - **Gabriel "Gah-bé" Vanaver**
Little Fish - **Bridget Law**
Water Spirit - **Xerephine**

Musical Performance by The Front Range Strings
feat. **Darren Garvey** (percussion)

Arrangement by **Phil Norman**